INTERFACT ™

THE BOOK AND DISK THAT WORK TOGETHER

VOLCANOES

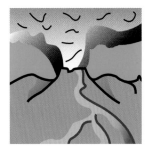

TWO CAN ™

MINNETONKA, MINNESOTA

Book and disk by
act-two Ltd

Published by Two-Can Publishing
11571 K-Tel Drive
Minnetonka, MN 55343
www.two-canpublishing.com

This edition Copyright © 2000 Two-Can Publishing

ISBN: 1-58728-468-5

2 4 6 8 10 9 7 5 3

Photographic Credits: Front cover Planet Earth Pictures
Ardea: p.24h, Bruce Colman. p.14b, Explorer: p.11, p.12/13, p.28; GeoScience Features Picture Library:
p.9, p.10/11, p.15r, p.19, p.23; Robert Harding Picture Library: p.15l; The Hutchinson Library: p.23r; Frank Lane Picture Agency Ltd:
p.12tr, p.14t; Rex Features: p.23t; Survival Anglia Photo Library: p.22 p.25tl; Zefa: p.18, p.20, p.24/25, p.25tr
All illustrations by Francis Mosley except those on pages 28–32 which are by Malcom Stokes of Linden Artists

Printed in China by WKT

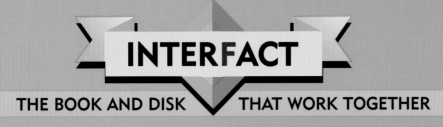

INTERFACT

THE BOOK AND DISK ▼ THAT WORK TOGETHER

INTERFACT will have you hooked in minutes –
and that's a fact!

The disk is full of interactive activities, puzzles, quizzes, and games that are fun to do and packed with interesting facts.

Drag the name tags around the screen and see if you can label all the parts of a volcano.

Open the book and discover more fascinating information highlighted with lots of full-color illustrations and photographs.

Where are the world's volcanoes found? Read and find out!

To get the most out of **INTERFACT**, use the book and disk together. Look for the special signs called Disk Links and Bookmarks. To find out more, turn to page 43.

23

BOOKMARK

DISK LINK
Vince and Vicky will answer your questions. Just Ask the Experts!

Once you've launched **INTERFACT**, you'll never look back.

LOAD UP!
Go to **page 40** to find out how to load your disks and click into action.

What's on the disk

HELP SCREEN

Learn how to use the disk in no time at all.

Welcome to the

INTERFACT

disk on Volcanoes

To have a look at all the different things on the disk, simply click the arrow keys with your mouse.

As you do this, you'll see a description of each activity in the text box.

Click on the picture at the top of the screen to select the activity you want to investigate.

These are the controls the Help Screen will tell you how to use:

- arrow keys
- text boxes
- "hot" words

A LOT ON YOUR PLATE

An interactive jigsaw puzzle made of the earth's plates!

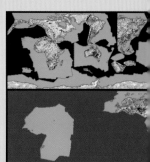

See if you can fit all of the earth's tectonic plates back together and mak
a map of the globe. Then learn about the movement of the plates and how it
causes volcanoes and earthquakes.

FANTASTIC FOUR

Take a look at the four types of eruptions!

With a click of your mouse, you can make four kinds of volcanoes erupt before your very eyes. Then investigate them in more detail and find out what happens inside each one.

MOUNTAINS OF FUN

Explore a virtual volcanic landscape!

Scientists who study volcanoes are called volcanologists. Their <u>shiny suits</u> reflect heat and allow them to work near the volcano's fiery furnace.

Investigate a volcanic landscape. Discover a lake inside a volcano, find a geyser, and learn how to recognize the different mountain shapes caused by various types of volcanoes.

ASK THE EXPERTS

Get the answers to some hot questions about volcanoes!

When it comes to volcanoes, there's nothing that Vince and Vicky don't know. Our expert volcanologists are waiting to answer all your questions. All you have to do is ask!

HOW MUCH DO YOU VOLCA-KNOW?

A quiz to test your knowledge of volcanoes!

Travel around the world, answering questions about volcanoes. If you complete the journey in time, you get to visit the sites of the world's most famous eruptions.

LAVA LABELS

Investigate the different parts of a volcano.

See if you can label the different parts of a volcano correctly. Drag the labels around the screen with your mouse. Once they are all in the correct position, learn more about each part.

DON'T BLOW IT!

Can you keep the volcano from erupting?

See if you can guess the mystery volcanic word before your time runs out. There's a volcano waiting to erupt on screen. Use your knowledge to save the day!

What's in the book

*All words in the text that appear in **bold** can be found in the glossary*

What is a volcano?

Volcanoes are openings in the surface of the earth from which gas and hot rock escape and cover the surrounding land. Some volcanoes are simply long cracks in the ground. Others are cone-shaped mountains with a hole in the top. This hole is called a **vent**.

While molten rock is inside the earth, it is known as **magma**. But when it escapes to the earth's surface, it is called **lava**. As lava flows away from the vent, it cools and hardens. Layers of lava, ash, and cinders from the volcano pile up to creat the **cone**.

DISK LINK
Play Lava Labels and see if you can name all the parts of a volcano.

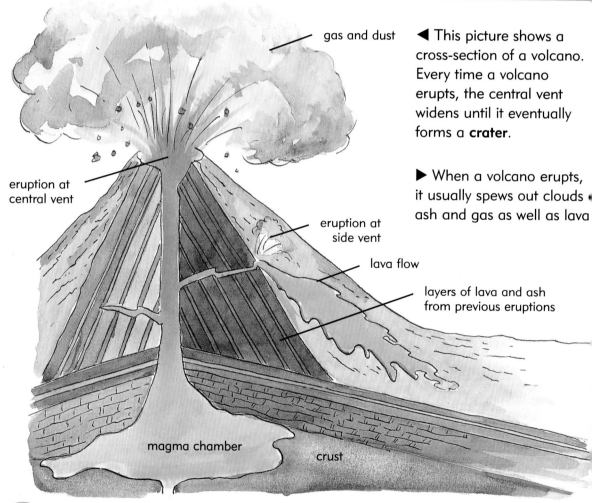

gas and dust

◀ This picture shows a cross-section of a volcano. Every time a volcano erupts, the central vent widens until it eventually forms a **crater**.

▶ When a volcano erupts, it usually spews out clouds ash and gas as well as lava

eruption at central vent

eruption at side vent

lava flow

layers of lava and ash from previous eruptions

magma chamber

crust

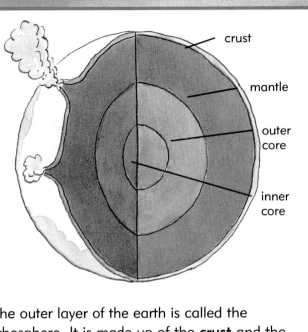

crust

mantle

outer core

inner core

The outer layer of the earth is called the lithosphere. It is made up of the **crust** and the solid top part of the **mantle**. The lithosphere is split into vast slabs called **plates**. Plates float on the layer of liquid rock that makes up the rest of the mantle. Below the mantle is a layer of molten metals called the outer **core**. In the middle is the inner core, which is made up mostly of solid iron.

Volcanic eruptions

Volcanic eruptions are spectacular and often terrifying sights. There are different types of volcanic eruptions. Sometimes, red-hot lava will shoot hundreds of yards or meters into the air, creating deadly fire fountains. Other times, it will pour down the sides of a mountain in fiery rivers. These lava streams can travel great distances, burning, burying, or flattening anything in their path. Some volcanoes emit burning-hot clouds of gas. Others explode, sending out dusty, hot ash and **volcanic bombs**.

▶ This lava flow from Mauna Loa, one of Hawaii's many volcanoes, is very runny. It will travel a long way before it cools and hardens.

▼ Fire fountains erupt from twin cones on Mount Etna, on the island of Sicily. Red-hot lava flows down to the mountain's base.

DISK LINK
Investigate the different types of eruptions in Fantastic Four!

DID YOU KNOW?

● Stromboli, off the coast of Italy, is one of the few volcanoes in Europe that is constantly **active**. It regularly emits clouds of dust.

● On average, between 20 and 30 volcanoes erupt each year.

● Mauna Loa, on Hawaii, is the largest active volcano on earth. One eruption lasted one-and-a-half years!

● The volcanoes on Hawaii, like the one in the diagram below, have wide, gently sloping cones. The runny lava from these volcanoes flows and spreads so quickly that the cones do not grow to great heights.

Going out with a bang

Sometimes, magma is stiff and thick and it hardens inside a volcano. Pressure builds up behind the blockage because gases in the magma below cannot escape. Often, the pressure becomes so great that a huge explosion takes place. When this type of eruption occurs, the whole mountain may be blown apart. Following the explosion, the center of the volcano may collapse into its own magma chamber, creating a large, circular crater called a **caldera**.

▶ Violent eruptions can shoot out huge clouds of ash that bury the surrounding countryside, killing animals, plants, and even people.

DISK LINK
One of the words on the previous page may help your chances in Don't Blow It!

Volcanic materials

Different volcanoes produce different types of lava. Lava can be runny or thick. Some volcanoes produce no lava. They shoot out solid pieces of rock. The tiniest pieces are known as **volcanic dust**. The largest ones are called volcanic bombs.

Dust from volcanoes can cover huge areas. Particles of volcanic dust in the atmosphere sometimes produce brilliant red sunsets across the globe.

Volcanoes also produce clouds of steam and gases. These clouds can rush down the mountain at more than 96 miles (160 km) per hour.

DISK LINK
Vince and Vicky can answer all your questions about lava. All you have to do is Ask the Experts!

▲ This huge area of hardened lava is known as a lava field.

▼ This valley is covered in a thick layer of volcanic dust. As it is washed into the ground, the dust makes the soil fertile.

▲ **Pumice** is a type of volcanic rock that is formed when lava cools very quickly. It is full of tiny air pockets and is light enough to float in water.

▲ As lava cools, it hardens and forms unusual patterns on the ground. Runny lava produces this wrinkled surface known as **pahoehoe** (say pah-HO-ee-ho-ee).

Where volcanoes are found

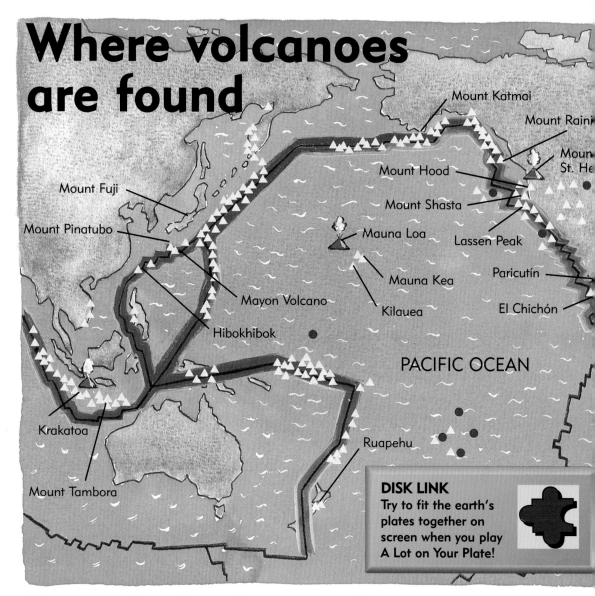

Mount Katmai

Mount Rain[i]

Moun[t] St. He[...]

Mount Hood

Mount Fuji

Mount Shasta

Mauna Loa

Lassen Peak

Mount Pinatubo

Mauna Kea

Paricutín

Mayon Volcano

Kilauea

El Chichón

Hibokhibok

PACIFIC OCEAN

Krakatoa

Ruapehu

Mount Tambora

DISK LINK
Try to fit the earth's plates together on screen when you play A Lot on Your Plate!

The earth's hard outer layers – the crust and the upper mantle – are divided into huge, moving pieces called plates. These can be up to 45 miles (75 km) thick. They float on the molten rock in the mantle.

Volcanoes form along ridges where plates move apart. They also occur where two plates collide and one is forced beneath the other. This happens in the

▲ This map shows the earth's plates and the location of many volcanoes.

so-called **Ring of Fire** around the Pacific Ocean. Other volcanoes, such as those i[n] Hawaii, lie far from the plate edges. The[y] form over **hot spots** – areas of fierce hea[t] in the mantle that cause magma to bubble up toward the surface.

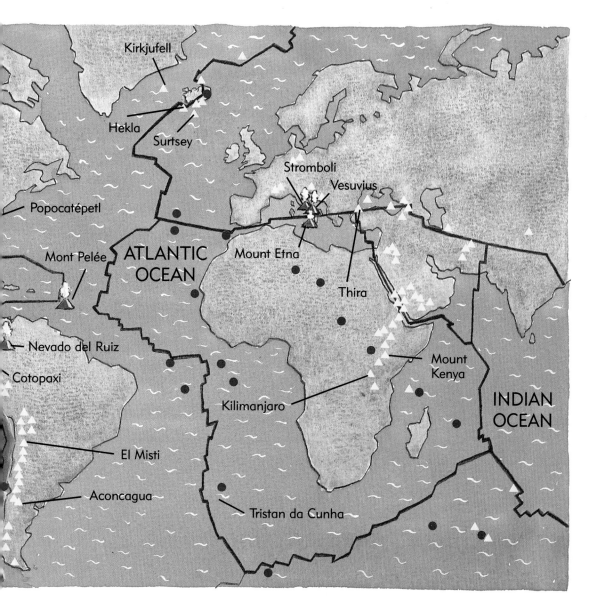

Kirkjufell

Hekla

Surtsey

Stromboli

Vesuvius

Popocatépetl

Mont Pelée

ATLANTIC
OCEAN

Mount Etna

Thira

Nevado del Ruiz

Cotopaxi

Mount
Kenya

INDIAN
OCEAN

Kilimanjaro

El Misti

Aconcagua

Tristan da Cunha

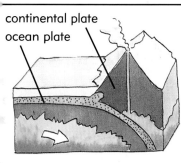

continental plate

ocean plate

When an ocean plate collides with a continental plate, it is forced down under the land mass and starts to melt. This forms magma that rises through the continental plate to create volcanoes.

Key to Map

Volcano

Hot spot

Direction of plate movement

Plate boundary

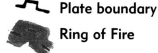

Ring of Fire

Volcanic islands

Some of the earth's most spectacular scenery lies beneath the waves. Deep trenches cut the sea floor, sweeping valleys stretch for miles, and great mountain ranges rise from the ocean floor. Many of these mountains are volcanoes.

When an underwater volcano erupts, the lava hardens as it meets the water. Repeated eruptions may cause the volcano's top to emerge from the sea.

In 1963, the crew of a fishing boat off the coast of Iceland saw a column of smoke in the distance. As they sailed

▼ White Island is a volcanic island. It lies off the eastern coast of New Zealand's North Island, in an area called the Bay of Plenty. A number of similar volcanic islands are scattered around New Zealand's coastline.

As an underwater volcano erupts, it spews lava that cools and hardens. A cone-shaped mountain forms around the vent.

The volcano grows with each eruption. Eventually, gas and lava rise above the waves, and the top of the volcano breaks the surface of the water.

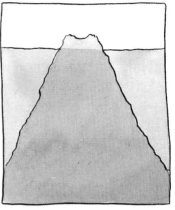

The top of the volcano now lies above sea level. A volcanic island has been born.

closer, billowing clouds of ash and steam began to rise above the waves. The fishermen were witnessing the birth of a volcanic island!

As the tip of the new island broke the surface of the water, red-hot lava began to pour from dozens of vents in its cone. That night, the island was 36 feet (11 m) above sea level. Four days later, it was as tall as two houses and 2,133 feet (650 m) wide.

The island was named Surtsey, and scientists from all over the world came to study it. The scientists monitored the eruptions of the volcano and studied the growth of animal and plant life on the new island. Surtsey continued to grow and change for almost four years.

The last eruption on Surtsey was in 1967. The island now covers more than 1 square mile (2.6km²).

▼ Clouds of ash and steam pour out from one of the vents on Iceland's volcanic island of Surtsey.

Hot springs and geysers

The red-hot magma that creates volcanoes also can create **hot springs** and **geysers**. These are formed when water seeps down into rock above the magma chamber and is heated. The warm water bubbles back to the surface in the form of a hot spring or shoots upward as a jet of steam and hot water known as a geyser.

Some geysers erupt at regular intervals. A geyser's fountain of steam rises and falls because once the steam has escaped, the geyser refills with water and the process starts all over again.

If water is heated by a volcano and mixes with the soil, hot mud pools that boil and bubble on the earth's surface are produced.

▼ Some people believe that bathing in mud pools can cure certain illnesses.

▲ Yellowstone Park in Wyoming has more than 200 geysers.

DISK LINK
Find some hot springs and geysers on the disk. It's Mountains of Fun!

Make a volcano

You will need:

A small, empty, clean
bottle, such as an ink
bottle or perfume
bottle
A piece of cardboard
A pin
A small glass
Food coloring
Water

1. Fill the glass half
full of cold water.

2. Using the pin, make a small
hole in the center of the
cardboard.

3. Put four or five
drops of food coloring
into the bottle. Then fill
the bottle with hot water
from the tap.

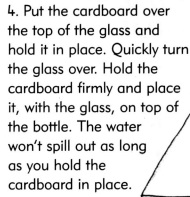

4. Put the cardboard over
the top of the glass and
hold it in place. Quickly turn
the glass over. Hold the
cardboard firmly and place
it, with the glass, on top of
the bottle. The water
won't spill out as long
as you hold the
cardboard in place.

5. Still holding the
cardboard, press down
gently on the glass. Puffs
of color will rise through
the pinhole into the glass.
(Warm water is lighter
than cold water, so the
warm water rises!)

Living near a volcano

Throughout history, people have lived near volcanoes. This can be dangerous, as in 1883, when the volcanic island of Krakatoa, in Indonesia, exploded. It set off a huge wave called a tsunami that drowned 36,000 people. The explosion was heard 2,900 miles (4,800 km) away.

Even when the eruption is not as violent, clouds of poisonous gas can still kill people and wildlife. In 1982, El Chichón, in Mexico, erupted. It released a cloud of sulfur dioxide, killing 187 people.

Lava flows can also engulf whole towns. In 1973, the town of Vestmannajyer on the island of Heimaey, Iceland, was buried under tons of red-hot lava when the Helgafell volcano erupted.

As well as dangers, there are also advantages to living near a volcano. Nutrient-rich volcanic soil is good for growing crops such as rice and potatoes. Many important minerals and metals, such as sulfur and copper, are mined from volcanic rocks.

DISK LINK
Remember what you read on these pages. It could come in handy when you play How Much Do You Volca-Know?

In 1985, volcanic mud swept through the city of Armero in Colombia, killing about 25,000 people.

The town of Vestmannajyer, Iceland, was overwhelmed by lava in 1973. The islanders sprayed the lava with seawater for five months to try to halt its flow.

Mineral-rich volcanic soil is perfect for growing rice. Farmers terrace the steep hillsides to prevent the valuable soil from being washed away by rain.

These Japanese macaques, or snow monkeys, live in the often freezing temperatures and snowy conditions of the high forests in Japan. They keep warm by bathing in hot volcanic springs.

Types of volcanoes

Volcanoes are classified as being active, **dormant,** or extinct. An active volcano is one that is erupting or may erupt in the future. When it is not erupting, an active volcano is said to be dormant. An extinct volcano is one that scientists believe will never erupt again.

After an eruption, an active volcano may go quiet for a long period. It appears to be just like any other mountain. Snow may settle on its summit, and there may be no signs of volcanic activity. An active volcano can remain dormant for many years. However, deep below the surface, the huge pressure of the magma can build up, and further eruptions may occur many years later.

When a volcano is truly extinct, the magma below it sinks back into the depths of the earth. Eventually, the weather wears away the cone until only the **volcanic plug** of solidified lava is left.

▲ Sometimes the cone of an active volcano collapses, forming a caldera. The caldera can fill with water, forming a circular lake, such as Crater Lake in Oregon, *above*. The island in the middle of the lake is a new volcanic cone.

DISK LINK
What type of volcano is Fuji? Find out in Mountains of Fun!

▲ Eroded volcanic craters on the Galapagos Islands in the Pacific Ocean provide unique wildlife habitats for creatures such as this land iguana.

▼ Mount Fuji, the highest mountain in Japan, last erupted in 1707.

▲ The chapel of St. Michel d'Aguiche in the French town of Le Puy sits on top of an 260-foot- (80-m-) high volcanic plug. This pillar of rock once filled the central channel of a volcano.

Science at work

For years, scientists have been developing ways of predicting volcanic eruptions, so that people living nearby have time to reach safety.

Before an eruption, there are often small underground earthquakes caused by the magma splitting rocks apart as it rises to the surface. An instrument called a **seismometer** helps scientists pinpoint the exact position of the rising magma. Near Kilauea, in Hawaii, this technique has been so successful that scientists have been able to predict the times and places of eruptions accurately.

In the scientific observatory near Mount Etna, scientists can actually hear the magma pouring through vents within the volcano. As it does so, it makes a sort of singing sound. By listening to this noise, scientists can follow the magma's movements and try to predict which of

▼ Scientists who study volcanoes are called volcanologists. When they are observing an erupting volcano, they have to wear special heat-resistant suits.

the volcano's vents it might break through during the next eruption.

When magma pushes up from below, the sides of a volcano may begin to bulge. This causes the ground to swell and tilt. The angle of the ground can be measured using an instrument called a **tiltmeter**. Again, this helps scientists to tell where an eruption is going to occur.

Studying volcanic ash and rocks can reveal a lot about previous eruptions. Scientists can figure out how big they were, how long they lasted, and what areas they affected. It is even possible to calculate the time between previous eruptions and predict when the next eruption might occur.

DISK LINK
One of the words on this page could help stop a volcanic eruption. So, Don't Blow It!

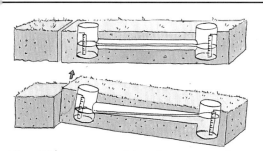

The tiltmeter consists of two containers set several yards or meters apart and joined by a tube. If the ground tilts, liquid runs from one container to the other. The change in the levels of the liquid indicates the angle of tilt.

DID YOU KNOW?

● Scientists believe that volcanic eruptions can cause changes in the weather. The eruption of Mount Tambora, near Java, in 1816 was blamed for freezing, wintery weather in the middle of summer in Europe and the United States. Americans nicknamed the year "Eighteen hundred and froze-to-death."

● The heat inside the earth that causes volcanoes can often be put to good use. Many houses in Reykjavik, Iceland, are heated by hot water that is piped from underground springs. Power plants in New Zealand, Italy, the United States, Japan, Mexico, and Chile use volcanic steam to generate electricity. Energy from these hot zones is known as **geothermal** energy.

Birth of a volcano

Dionisio Pulido was a farmer in Mexico. He worked the land, as his father and grandfather had done before him. But, in 1943, something started growing in his fields – and it wasn't corn! This is the true story of what happened.

Dionisio Pulido awoke with a start. Dawn was breaking and sunlight was streaming through the tiny window above his bed. Dionisio lay for a moment, watching, listening, and trying to figure out what had interrupted his sleep. Suddenly, the walls of his hut began to tremble. The floor creaked and groaned as the old wooden planks were disturbed. Even his bed seemed to be moving.

Dionisio murmured a silent prayer, asking God to protect him, his family, and all the villagers.

It was February 20, 1943. For 15 days now, the Mexican village of Paricutín, where Dionisio lived, had been vibrating with small earthquakes.

Each day, the tremors had become a little stronger and more frequent. In one day alone there had been more than 500! The villagers were very frightened.

As soon as the tremors stopped, Dionisio jumped out of bed and headed off to his fields, close to the village. He had planned to plow his cornfield that day, to get it ready for planting. He must try to put the earthquakes out of his mind. He had work to do!

Dionisio hitched his oxen to the plow and set to work. It was a bitterly cold day, but Dionisio noticed that the soil beneath his feet felt quite warm. At first this puzzled him, but he soon forgot about it as the hard work of plowing began to make him feel tired and sore.

In one corner of the field there was an outcrop of rock with a small hollow in it. This hollow had been there for as long as Dionisio could remember, and the village children often played in it.

As Dionisio neared that corner of the field in the late afternoon, he noticed a large crack in the ground by the rock.

It was about 80 feet (25 m) long, and went straight through the hollow.

Dionisio walked forward to look at the crack more carefully. As he did so, he heard a loud, rumbling sound, like thunder, that seemed to come from beneath his feet. Smoke began to rise from the hollow, and the trees at the edge of the field began to sway.

Suddenly, the ground around the rock split wide open and bulged up. Dionisio ran as if the devil was after him! He had no idea that he had just seen the birth of a volcano.

Dionisio raced into the village, shouting at the top of his voice. The villagers

gathered quickly to find out what had happened. Dionisio pointed to his field. In the distance, they could now see red-hot rock emerging from a hole at the end of the crack. This hole grew bigger and bigger as they watched.

Some of the villagers stayed up all night, fearful yet fascinated at the same time. Others prayed in the church. At 8 a.m. the next day, Dionisio went back to his cornfield. He found that a 30-foot- (10-m-) high cone had grown overnight – and it was still growing! By midday, the cone was about 150 feet (45 m) high, and by nightfall, red-hot lava was pouring slowly from its vent. The next morning, Dionisio realized that he had no field left!

That day, those villagers who had not already fled decided it was time to escape. They were just in time! By the end of one week, the volcano had grown to a height of 460 feet (140 m). Fragments of rock were thrown almost 4 miles (6 km) into the air, and the noise of the explosions could be heard in Mexico City, 490 miles (816 km) away.

As the villagers left, scientists began to

arrive from all over the world to watch and study this new volcano. The village of Paricutín and the nearby village of San Juan Parangaricútiru were both destroyed. Vast quantities of volcanic ash covered the countryside for 7 miles (12 km) around. Only the top of the church in San Juan Parangaricútiru could be seen above the lava. Cattle grew thin and died because all the grass was buried under a thick carpet of ash. Water was scarce because the rivers were choked with rocks. Birds, overcome by poisonous gases, dropped from the sky, dead.

The volcano kept erupting and growing. Then in 1952, nine years after its dramatic birth, it grew calm. When Dionisio Pulido brought his grandchildren to visit the spot where his cornfield had once grown, the cone of volcanic debris towered 1,345 feet (410 m) above his cornfield. What a story he had to tell them!

True or false?

Which of these facts are true and which are false?
If you have read this book carefully, you will know the answers!

1. All volcanoes are cone-shaped mountains.

2. The Ring of Fire is a volcano in Hawaii.

3. Scientists who study volcanoes are called volcanologists.

4. The center of the earth is known as the crust.

5. Lava is the name given to magma when it erupts out of a volcano.

6. Rice and other food crops grow well in volcanic soil.

7. Volcanic dust can cause red sunsets.

8. Stromboli is the largest active volcano on earth.

9. A caldera is another name for a magma chamber.

10. The earth's hard outer layer is divided into plates.

11. As runny lava cools and hardens, it produces a wrinkled rock known as pahoehoe.

12. A dormant volcano is one that is not expected to erupt again.

13. Volcanic bombs are large pieces of rock that are sometimes thrown out during a volcanic eruption.

ANSWERS: 1.F 2.F 3.T 4.F 5.T 6.T 7.T 8.F 9.F 10.T 11.T 12.F 13.T

Glossary

Active is the word used to describe a volcano that erupts regularly.

Caldera is a huge, round crater that forms when the core of a volcano collapses inward.

Cone is a mountain that builds up around a volcano. It is made up of hardened lava as well as the ash and cinders that are thrown out of the volcano during an eruption.

Core is the name given to the center of the earth. It is divided into the outer core, which is made of hot liquid metals, and the inner core, which is mainly iron.

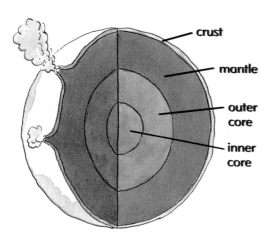

crust
mantle
outer core
inner core

Crater is the hole at the top of a volcano's vent. It may contain a lake.

Crust is the earth's thin, rocky surface layer. The crust and the top layer of the mantle are made up of huge, thick slabs of rock, called plates, that move around.

Dormant is the word used to describe an active volcano when it is not erupting.

Geothermal energy is energy that is obtained from the volcanic areas, or "hot zones," below the surface of the earth.

Geyser is a natural underground spring that shoots jets of steam and hot water into the air.

steam
geyser
porous rock
↑ heat source ↑

Hot spot is an area of fierce heat in the earth's mantle where magma bubbles up to the surface and forms a volcano.

Hot springs contain warm or hot water that bubbles to the earth's surface.

Lava is the name given to the magma inside the earth that escapes to the earth's surface.

Magma is the name given to the hot, liquid rock inside the earth.

Mantle is the layer of rock inside the earth, below the crust. It is partly molten.

Pahoehoe is the wrinkled, ropelike rock produced by runny lava as it cools and hardens.

Plate is one of the huge, thick slabs of rock that make up earth's outer layers.

Pumice is a very light type of rock that can float in water. It is formed when lava cools very quickly.

Ring of Fire is the name of a narrow zone that almost encircles the Pacific Ocean. This is where a large number of the world's active volcanoes are found.

Seismometer is an instrument that can pinpoint the position of rising magma. It is used by scientists to help predict where and when a volcano is going to erupt.

Tiltmeter is an instrument that measures the angle of the ground. The tilt is caused by magma pushing up from underground, making the sides of a volcano swell. This instrument can help scientists predict where an eruption will occur.

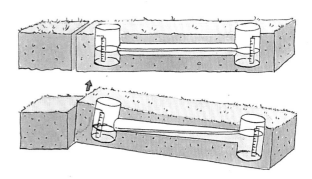

Vent is an opening in a volcano through which magma flows. The main vent is usually in the center of a volcano, but sometimes there are also vents in the sides of a volcano.

Volcanic bombs are the largest pieces of rock that shoot out of a volcano during an eruption.

Volcanic dust is the name given to the smallest pieces of rock that are thrown out of a volcano.

Volcanic plug is the piece of solid volcanic rock that remains after wind and water have worn away a volcano's cone over thousands or millions of years.

Lab pages

Photocopy these sheets and use them to make your own notes.

Loading your INTERFACT disk

INTERFACT is easy to load. But, before you begin, quickly run through the checklist on the opposite page to ensure that your computer is ready to run the program.

Your INTERFACT CD-ROM will run on both PCs with Windows and on Apple Macs. To make sure that your computer meets the system requirements, check the list below.

SYSTEM REQUIREMENTS

PC
- 486DX2/66 Mhz Processor
- Windows 3.1, 3.11, 95, 98 (or later)
- 8 Mb RAM (16 Mb recommended for Windows 95 and 24 Mb recommended for Windows 98)
- VGA colour monitor
- SoundBlaster-compatible soundcard

APPLE MACINTOSH
- 68020 processor
- system 7.0 (or later)
- 16 Mb of RAM

LOADING INSTRUCTIONS

You can run INTERFACT from the disk – you don't need to install it on your hard drive.

PC WITH WINDOWS 95 OR 98

The program should start automatically when you put the disk in the CD drive. If it does not, follow these instructions.

1. Put the disk in the CD drive
2. Open MY COMPUTER
3. Double-click on the CD drive icon
4. Double-click on the icon called VOLCANOES

PC WITH WINDOWS 3.1 OR 3.11

1. Put the disk in the CD drive
2. Select RUN from the FILE menu in the PROGRAM MANAGER
3. Type D:\VOLCANOES (Where D is the letter of your CD drive)
4. Press the RETURN key

APPLE MACINTOSH

1. Put the disk in the CD drive
2. Double click on the INTERFACT icon
3. Double click on the VOLCANOES icon

CHECKLIST

● Firstly, make sure that your computer and monitor meet the system requirements as set out on page 40.

● Ensure that your computer, monitor and CD-ROM drive are all switched on and working normally.

● It is important that you do not have any other applications, such as wordprocessors, running. Before starting INTERFACT quit all other applications.

● Make sure that any screen savers have been switched off.

● If you are running INTERFACT on a PC with Windows 3.1 or 3.11, make sure that you type in the correct instructions when loading the disk, using a colon (:) not a semi-colon (;) and a back slash (\) not a forward slash (/). Also, do not use any other punctuation or put any spaces between letters.

How to use INTERFACT

INTERFACT is easy to use.
First find out how to load the program
(see page 40), then read these simple
instructions and dive in!

**You will find that there are lots of
different features to explore.**
To select one, operate the controls
on the right-hand side of the screen.
You will see that the main area of
the screen changes as you click
on different features.

For example, this is what your
screen looks like when you play
Ask the Experts, where Vince
and Vicky are waiting to answer
all your questions. Once you've
selected a feature, click on the
main screen to start playing.

Are all mountains volcanoes?

ANSWER

Click here to select the feature you want to play.

Click on the Answer button, or ask another question.

Click on the arrow keys to scroll through the different features on the disk or find your way to the exit.

This is the text box, where instructions and directions appear. See page 4 to find out what's on the disk.

DISK LINKS

When you read the book, you'll come across Disk Links. These show you where to find activities on the disk that relate to the page you are reading. Use the arrow keys to find the icon on screen that matches the one in the Disk Link.

DISK LINK
Try to fit earth's plates together on screen when you play A Lot on Your Plate!

BOOKMARKS

As you explore the features on the disk, you'll bump into Bookmarks. These show you where to look in the book for more information about the topic on screen. Just turn to the page of the book shown in the Bookmark.

23

LAB PAGES

On pages 36 – 39, you'll find pages to photocopy. These are for making notes and recording any thoughts or ideas you may have as you read the book.

HOT DISK TIPS

• After you have chosen the feature you want to play, remember to move the cursor from the icon to the main screen before clicking the mouse again.

• If you don't know how to use one of the on-screen controls, simply touch it with your cursor. An explanation will pop up in the text box!

• Keep a close eye on the cursor. When it changes from an arrow ➜ to a hand, 👆 click your mouse and something will happen.

• Any words that appear on screen in blue and underlined are "hot." This means you can touch them with the cursor for more information.

• Explore the screen! There are secret hot spots and hidden surprises to find.

Troubleshooting

If you come across a problem loading or running the INTERFACT disk, you should find the solution here. If you still cannot solve your problem, send us an email at helpline@two-canpublishing.com.

QUICK FIXES Run through these general checkpoints before consulting COMMON PROBLEMS (see opposite page).

(see opposite page)

QUICK FIXES — PC WITH WINDOWS 3.1 OR 3.11

1 Check that you have the minimum system requirements: 386/33Mhz, VGA color monitor, 4Mb of RAM.

2 Make sure you have typed in the correct instructions: a colon (:) not a semi-colon (;) and a back slash (\) not a forward slash (/). Also, do not put any spaces between letters or punctuation.

3 It is important that you do not have any other programs running. Before you start **INTERFACT**, hold down the Control key and press Escape. If you find that other programs are open, click on them with the mouse, then click the End Task key.

QUICK FIXES — PC WITH WINDOWS 95

1 Make sure you have typed in the correct instructions: a colon (:) not a semi-colon (;) and a back slash(\) not a forward slash (/). Also, do not put any spaces between letters or punctuation.

2 It is important that you do not have any other programs running. Before you start **INTERFACT**, look at the task bar. If you find that other programs are open, click with the right mouse button and select Close from the pop-up menu.

MACINTOSH

1 Make sure that you have the minimum system requirements: 68020 processor, 640x480 color display, system 7.0 (or a later version), and 4Mb of RAM.

2 It is important that you do not have any other programs running. Before you start **INTERFACT**, click on the application menu in the top right-hand corner. Select each of the open applications and select Quit from the File menu.

COMMON PROBLEMS

Symptom: Cannot load disk.
Problem: There is not enough space available on your hard disk.
Solution: Make more space available by deleting old applications and files you don't use until 6Mb of free space is available.

Symptom: Disk will not run.
Problem: There is not enough memory available.
Solution: *Either* quit other open applications (see Quick Fixes) *or* increase your machine's RAM by adjusting the Virtual Memory.

Symptom: Graphics do not load or are of poor quality.
Problem: *Either* there is not enough memory available *or* you have the wrong display setting.
Solution: *Either* quit other applications (see Quick Fixes) *or* make sure that your monitor control is set to 640x480x256 or VGA.

Symptom: There is no sound (PCs only).
Problem: Your sound card is not Soundblaster compatible.
Solution: Try to configure your sound settings to make them Soundblaster compatible (refer to your sound card manual for more details).

Symptom: Your machine freezes.
Problem: There is not enough memory available.
Solution: *Either* quit other applications (see Quick Fixes) *or* increase your machine's RAM by adjusting the Virtual Memory.

Symptom: Text does not fit neatly into boxes and "hot" copy does not bring up extra information.
Problem: Standard fonts on your computer have been moved or deleted.
Solution: Reinstall standard fonts. The PC version requires Arial; the Macintosh version requires Helvetica. See your computer manual for further information.

Index

▲ Eroded volcanic craters on the Galapagos Islands in the Pacific Ocean provide unique wildlife habitats for creatures such as this land iguana.

▼ Mount Fuji, the highest mountain in Japan, last erupted in 1707.

▲ The chapel of St. Michel d'Aguiche in the French town of Le Puy sits on top of an 260-foot- (80-m-) high volcanic plug. This pillar of rock once filled the central channel of a volcano.

Science at work

For years, scientists have been developing ways of predicting volcanic eruptions, so that people living nearby have time to reach safety.

Before an eruption, there are often small underground earthquakes caused by the magma splitting rocks apart as it rises to the surface. An instrument called

▼ Scientists who study volcanoes are called volcanologists. When they are observing an erupting volcano, they have to wear special heat-resistant suits.

a **seismometer** helps scientists pinpoint the exact position of the rising magma. Near Kilauea, in Hawaii, this technique has been so successful that scientists have been able to predict the times and places of eruptions accurately.

In the scientific observatory near Mount Etna, scientists can actually hear the magma pouring through vents within the volcano. As it does so, it makes a sort of singing sound. By listening to this noise, scientists can follow the magma's movements and try to predict which of